That Grand Master Jumping Teacher,
BERNARD, MEETS JEROME,
the Great Jumping Glump

THAT GRAND MASTER JUMPING TEACHER, BERNARD, MEETS JEROME, THE GREAT JUMPING GLUMP

Story and Pictures by
David McPhail

FREDERICK WARNE
New York London

For my brother,
BERNARD

Copyright © 1982 by David McPhail
All rights reserved. No part of this book may be
reproduced or transmitted in any form or by any means
without permission in writing from the publisher, except
for brief quotations used in connection with reviews written
specifically for inclusion in a magazine or newspaper.
Frederick Warne & Co., Inc.
New York, New York
Library of Congress Cataloging in Publication Data
McPhail, David M.
That grand master jumping teacher, Bernard,
meets Jerome, the great jumping glump.
Summary: Bernard, who has been jumping since before
he was born, opens a school where he coaches
Jerome for the world championship jumping match.
[1. Jumping—Fiction]   I. Title.
PZ7.M2427Tg   [E]   81-16507
ISBN 0-7232-6209-8   AACR2
Printed in the U.S.A. by
Typography by Kathleen Westray
1 2 3 4 5 86 85 84 83 82

BERNARD

Bernard was a good jumper, even before he was born.

"This baby certainly is a good jumper!" Bernard's mother would say. Then Bernard's father would put his hand on Bernard's mother's tummy and say, "This baby is a good jumper, all right. No doubt about that!"

Bernard loved to jump. When he was just a few months old he jumped right out of his crib, even though the mattress had been lowered almost to the floor.

Once, at the dinner table, Bernard jumped out of his high chair and landed in the soup tureen. "No more jumping at the table!" scolded Bernard's father.

For Bernard's fourth birthday his mother made him a jumping costume. It had a blue satin cape and velvet jumping boots.

He wore the costume nearly all the time, but sometimes it got dirty and had to be washed. When that happened, Bernard just wasn't himself until his costume was cleaned and dry, and he was wearing it again.

When Bernard was not sleeping or eating, he was jumping. He jumped up, and he jumped down. (And landed as softly as a feather floating to earth.)

Bernard jumped forward, backward, and sideways.

He could do twists and spins, flips and flops.

He could jump across his bedroom without ever being more than two inches from the floor.

Bernard could jump over three dump trucks parked end to end.

He could outjump Joey Baker's bullfrog by half a mile.

Besides being a superb jumper, Bernard was a wonderful person, and everyone who knew him loved him very much. He was kind and sincere and fun to be with. Bernard was dependable, too, and could always be counted on to return his library books on time, even if it meant going out in inclement weather.

Bernard was also very brave, and his heroic acts were widely known. Once he jumped onto a railroad trestle and snatched a baby possum from the path of a highballing freight train (which is not something that just anyone should try).

One day Bernard decided to open a jumping school. He built a small studio and hung out a sign that read: *Studio of Bernard, Grand Master Jumping Teacher.*

THE JUMPING SCHOOL

Bernard's jumping school was a marvelous place. The floor was slightly padded, and the roof, which was attached to the wall with giant hinges, could be swung open to the sky. Two of the walls were lined with mirrors, and a third was covered with inspirational photographs of jumpers in action.

Against the fourth wall were bookcases that housed Bernard's rather extensive collection of jumping books, and carved in big block letters above the front door was Bernard's motto: *Joy Through Jumping.*

At the grand opening of his school, that Grand Master Bernard looked resplendent in his jumping costume, which had been cleaned and pressed just for the occasion.

During the day-long open house, which followed the ribbon-cutting ceremony, many people registered for jumping classes, especially after Bernard gave a modest demonstration of his remarkable jumping abilities. One of Bernard's first pupils was a retired automobile mechanic named Bertha Bettleton. Bertha was as large as some of the cars she had worked on, and she hoped that she might jump her way into a sleeker and slimmer chassis.

Bernard, of course, made no promises, nor gave any guarantees, but his enthusiasm and his concerned attention inspired Bertha and his other pupils to lofty achievements.

People wrote to Bernard from all over the world, asking his expert advice, and though the volume of mail was considerable, Bernard personally responded to each and every inquiry.

Bernard had many pupils. Some, like Bertha Bettleton, came to lose weight, while others came seeking peace of mind. Still others came because they loved to jump.

There were some, however, who had quite different reasons for coming to Bernard's jumping school. One such pupil, and the pupil that Bernard most fondly remembers, was Jerome, the Great Jumping Glump.

JEROME, THE GREAT JUMPING GLUMP

Jerome, the Great Jumping Glump was feel-ing low. The one thing he had always dreaded had finally happened. He had been challenged to a jumping contest by his archrival, Gerald, the Conceited Kangaroo. This would be Jerome's first defense of his title, and he was understandably nervous — especially when he remembered that he couldn't jump.

He could barely stand on his tiptoes. Even so, Jerome was the World's Champion Jumper. It was a title that he inherited from his father, who was also a great jumping Glump.

In desperation Jerome sought the advice and counsel of that Grand Master Jumping Teacher, Bernard. "You've got to teach me to jump," he pleaded. "If you don't, I'll be the laughingstock of the whole world."

"Let me see your style," Bernard said to Jerome.

"I have no style," confessed Jerome. "I can't jump! Not an inch. Not at all!"

Bernard loved a challenge, but this was ridiculous. The match with Gerald was scheduled for the following Tuesday, and this was Friday. So he sent Jerome home with instructions that he do certain exercises every night before going to bed.

"Without fail!" said Bernard sternly. "And report back to me on Monday morning!"

That night Jerome stood in front of his full-length mirror and performed the exercises Bernard had recommended.

Holding onto the bedpost for balance, Jerome attempted to raise himself up on the balls of his feet ten times.

"...six...seven...eight..." puffed Jerome. Then he tried a deep knee bend. *Kerplumpf!* Jerome fell into a heap on the floor.

"It's no use," Jerome reported to Bernard on Monday morning.

"Forget the knee bends," said Bernard. "Let me see you do the toe raises."

With a firm grip on the ballet bar, Jerome began his exercise routine. "... six ... seven ... eight ..." he puffed.

"What happened to nine and ten?" asked Bernard.

"I can't do them," said Jerome.

"You must!" scolded Bernard. "If you are ever going to jump you must do nine and ten!"

Jerome's muscles quivered as he struggled to continue. Up! Up! Up!

"Ohhhh," moaned Jerome as he came crashing down.

But instead of staying down, he bounced back up! Then down . . . then up again! And this time his feet actually left the floor! He had jumped! Or had he bounced?

To Jerome it didn't matter in the least. He continued to go up and down, higher and higher, until his head was bumping against Bernard's ceiling.

"That's wonderful!" said Bernard, and he grabbed hold of Jerome to make him stop.

"I did it!" cried Jerome. "I jumped!"

"You certainly did," confirmed Bernard as he intensely examined the bottom of Jerome's feet.

"Amazing!" he exclaimed. "Your feet feel like they are made of rubber!"

"That must be the secret," said Jerome. "The secret of the great jumping Glumps. All of the world's champion jumping Glumps probably have had rubber feet! That's what my father was trying to tell me when he lost control at the last world's championship contest and jumped right through the sky."

"You'd better go home and get some sleep," suggested Bernard. "Tomorrow you meet Gerald, the Conceited Kangaroo, to decide who is the best jumper in the world."

THE CONTEST

Jerome slept soundly that night and woke the next morning to the pip pip pip of raindrops on his windowsill. He showered and dressed, and then he went to meet Bernard at the park where the contest was to be held.

Gerald, the Conceited Kangaroo was already there, dazzling the crowd with the trick of balancing on his tail.

Bernard was checking out the official jumping platform.

"Seems sturdy enough," he said to Jerome. "But the rain has made the surface a bit slippery."

At ten o'clock, Captain Toad, the official referee, called the two contestants onto the platform.

"For the jumping championship of the world," he announced.

"The challenger, Gerald . . . and the champion Jerome!"

"Each contestant will have ten jumps," continued Captain Toad.

"The challenger will go first, and after each jump the champion must elect to jump or to pass. Whoever jumps the highest will be declared the winner. May the best jumper win!"

Gerald stepped forward and bowed to the crowd. Then with a flick of his tail he jumped ten feet in the air! The crowd ooh'd and ahh'd then hushed to await Jerome's response.

"I pass," said Jerome, yawning.

The crowd ooh'd and ahh'd again.

Gerald flexed his knees ever so slightly and shot like a rocket fifteen feet straight up.

"Hooray!" the crowd roared.

"I pass again," said Jerome.

Gerald slowly rocked back on his tail. TWANG! It was as though a huge slingshot had propelled him to a height of twenty-five feet.

"Still pass," said Jerome.

Now Captain Toad came over to have a few words with Jerome.

"When are you gonna make a jump?" asked the Captain.

"When that kangaroo is finished," replied Jerome.

Captain Toad relayed this information to Gerald, who in three short leaps was face to face with Jerome.

"That's three more jumps," said Bernard.

"Those three don't count!" Gerald shrieked.

"Indeed they do!" corrected Captain Toad. "Any jumps made during the contest shall be considered official jumps! Rule number 39!"

Gerald was seething. "I don't believe you *can* jump, Glump!" said Gerald, his face turning crimson.

"Four jumps is more than I'll need to beat this jumpless Glump!" shouted Gerald from the top of a thirty-foot leap.

On his next two jumps he went even higher, but on his final attempt Gerald slipped on a wet spot, landed right on his head, and remained there.

The crowd hooted and hollered.

Captain Toad bent over Gerald and said: "That was all very fine, immensely so. And it's a pity that no consideration can be given for style, acrobatic ability, and balance. Height is all we're after here. Height is all that matters!"

Now it was Jerome's chance to show why he was called the Great Jumping Glump, Champion Jumper of the World!

A final word of encouragement from his friend and teacher, Bernard, and Jerome was ready to begin.

He rocked back slowly onto his heels then fell forward onto the balls of his feet, and as he did so, the great bulk of the Glump rose ever so slightly off the platform. Then down, then up again! And each jump took him several times higher than the previous one.

Murmurs from the crowd became a hum which soon turned into a dull roar as more and more people got caught up in the excitement.

The platform creaked and groaned and the ground trembled as Jerome continued to jump.

"... five ... six ..." the crowd chanted, "... seven ... eight ..."

On his seventh jump Jerome surpassed Gerald's best effort by twelve feet! All that remained was to see how high he could go.

"... nine ..."

"... ten!"

Dressed in his yellow jump suit with the green racing stripe, Jerome resembled an enormous balloon just set loose from its moorings.

Like a great golden sun, Jerome went streaking
up through the sky.

"So long," called Bernard with a tear in his eye.
"So long Jerome, World's Champion Jumper!"

Several hours later, Bernard was still there, standing on the jumping platform. He was alone, very much alone. Everyone else had left long ago.

Bernard's neck was stiff and cramped from looking skyward for so long. He knew in his heart that Jerome wouldn't be back — he was gone forever.

Yet Bernard remained. Some unexplained feeling kept him there.

It grew dark and the moon shone brighter and brighter. As Bernard stared, he thought for an instant that he saw a tiny speck appear, silhouetted against the golden glow of the rising moon. Bernard blinked, and when he looked again, the speck was gone.

Suddenly Bernard dashed across the platform and leaped high into the air.

"For you, Jerome," he said softly.

Then he stepped down off the platform and walked slowly back to his studio to prepare the following day's lessons.